# Almost A Woman

## By
## Mary Wood Allen

# Almost A Woman

## CHAPTER I.

"Mother." The clear girlish voice rang through the house with persistent intensity but awakened no responsive call. Mr. Wayne, coming up the steps, heard the repeated summons for "Mother" and sent out his answering cry, "Father's here." Quick, light steps answered his call and an urgent young voice demanded, "Where's mother?"

"Mother has been called away for tonight, so you'll have to put up with father."

"O, dear!" sighed the girl despondently.

"Is father such a poor substitute, then?" inquired Mr. Wayne in an aggrieved tone.

"O, no," responded Helen, quickly. "You're usually as good as mother; but there were some special things I wanted to ask her about this evening. I suppose I can wait," she added, dolorously.

"Try me and see if I won't answer tolerably well. What are these weighty problems?" drawing his daughter to his knee as he spoke.

"That's it," pouted Helen. "You always make fun,—mother doesn't."

"Pardon me, daughter, I had no intention of making fun. I only wanted you to feel at home with me. It was a clumsy attempt, I'll admit, but really and truly I would like to be in your confidence—to feel that you trust me, too. I can't fill mother's place, I know, but I can do what mother can't, I can give you the man's view of things, and that is sometimes of great value for a girl to know."

"Yes," said Helen, snuggling down in her father's lap, for they were great friends and she felt his sympathy. "I often wish we could know how things look to other people. I know boys don't look at matters as girls do, but we can't always tell just what they do think."

"That is true," replied Mr. Wayne, gravely. "I often think that if girls knew just what boys say among themselves it would make them more careful of their conduct.

"For instance, not long ago I was on a steamer where there was dancing. I went into the smoking room, and there I heard the comments of the young men. I am sure the girls had no idea how their dress, figures, freedom and flirtatiousness were criticised and laughed at by these young men, who seemed to them, doubtless, so very nice and polite. Of course, these girls were mostly strangers to the young men and were getting acquainted without introductions, probably thinking it fine fun.”

“Yes, father. I’ve heard some of the real nice girls talk about getting acquainted in that way, and they seem to think it all right. Someway, it never seemed quite nice to me.”

“I hope not, my daughter. I should be sorry to have you form acquaintances in that way. You never can tell what a man’s character is by his clothes or manners. Indeed, you may think you know a man pretty well, and yet be mistaken. I suppose girls who are familiar with young men and allow them liberties imagine that they are trustworthy. I sat in front of two young men on a train not long ago. They appeared well and really were nice, as boys go, but they had the usual boy’s idea as to honor. They were talking freely of the girls they knew, discussing their merits and charms, saying that this one was soft and ‘huggable,’ that another was sweet to kiss—”

“O, father!” exclaimed Helen, in a fury of surprise and anger. “They didn’t talk that way so that you could hear! And call the girls by name, too?”

“Yes, they did, dear. Then after they had discussed several, who all seemed to allow great freedom, they mentioned another name, and their whole manner changed. ‘Ah,’ said one, ‘there’s no nonsense about her. It’s ‘hands off’ there every time and’—he went on, with great emphasis, ‘that’s the kind of a girl I mean to marry. A  man doesn’t want to feel that his wife’s been slobbered over by all the young men of her acquaintance.’”

Helen hid her face on her father’s shoulder. “How perfectly dreadful!” she said. “They were not gentlemen.”

“I’ll admit that,—and yet the conduct of the girls in permitting such freedom was really an excuse for their speaking so discourteously of them. The girls had not maintained their own self-respect, and therefore had not secured the respect of the young men. The girl who respected herself compelled respect from them, and that is the idea I wish to impress on your mind. Never expect any one to respect you more than you respect yourself, nor to shield your honor if you have placed yourself in their power.”

“But, father,” said Helen hesitatingly, “most of the girls and boys think it no harm to kiss each other good night, and the girls say the boys would be offended if a girl refused.”

“They are mistaken. Of course, the boys like to have the girls think so; but they don’t talk that way among themselves, you may be sure.”

"But, you see, father," urged Helen, hesitatingly, "they say they are engaged, and that makes it all right."

"How long do they stay engaged?" asked Mr. Wayne. "Do they really consider it a true engagement, to end ultimately in marriage, or is it merely an excuse for freedom of association?"

"O, they're all the time breaking their engagements. I don't believe they expect them to last very long. Now, there's Dora Ills. She's only sixteen and she says she's been engaged four times, and when she breaks the engagement she doesn't give back the ring. She's making a collection of engagement rings, she says."

"It is very evident that she cannot have the highest respect for herself. I knew of a girl whose sister had been engaged several times and who said to her, 'Why, Lida, you've never been engaged yet, have you?' And Lida replied, 'No, and I have made up my mind that I'll not be one of your pawed-over girls.'

"Her expression was not an elegant one, but it showed that she respected herself, and of course, she will be more truly respected by the young men if she does not permit them to approach too closely. A girl is very much mistaken if she fancies that a young man thinks more of her if she lets him be familiar. On the other hand, it is always true that he thinks more of her if she makes him feel that she is not to be carelessly approached. As one boy said to me, 'Girls ought to know that boys always want most that which is hardest to get.'"

"But, father, if it's so difficult for boys and girls to be together and act as they should, wouldn't it be best to keep them entirely apart until they are old enough to marry?"

"That is what they think in the old world, and  girls are kept shut up in schools and convents until they are grown; then their parents select a husband for them, and after they are married they are allowed to go into society. I am afraid our girls wouldn't like that,—they'd want to select their own husbands."

"They could do that after they got out of school."

"My observation is that the girl who has been shut up away from young men, is the very one who doesn't know how to act when she comes out of school. She has very romantic ideas, and is quite apt to be misled by a glittering exterior. She is less able to judge wisely or to guide her own conduct judiciously than the girl who, having been educated with boys, has less romantic ideas concerning them. No, I believe in co-education and in the common social life for both sexes; but with it I should ask that all young people should be taught to respect themselves and each other, and to understand their responsibility to future generations.”

“And what is that responsibility? What have we young people to do with future generations?”

“Just exactly what we older people once had. We didn’t think of it in our youth, but we can see now that even then we were creating our own characters and at the same time the characters of our future children. Now, I can see in you many of my own youthful characteristics. I can understand why you find it hard to do things that I’d  like you to do, and easy to do some I’d rather you wouldn’t do. And if, in the years to come, you have a daughter, she will be apt to be largely what you are now. All the efforts you make now to overcome your own faults are in reality helping to overcome those faults for her also. Suppose the young people knew and thought of these things; don’t you think they would judge more wisely of what they ought to do?”

“Why, yes, I know what I’d want my daughter to do, it seems to me, even better than I could tell what I ought to do myself.”

“Wouldn’t that be a good way to decide your own conduct—to do only those things which you’d be perfectly willing your daughter should do?”

“But, father, tell me why it’s so much more important for girls to be particular about what they do than for boys.”

“It’s not more important.”

“Well, people seem to think it is. The other day Johnnie Webster was going to a show and his little sister Carrie wanted to go, too, and he told her it was no place for girls, and she said, ‘Then it is no place for boys’; and he said, ‘But boys don’t have to be as good as girls.’ And his father and mother both heard it and never said a word. They only laughed.”

“It is unfortunately quite a common idea that boys and men do not have to be as good as girls and women; but it is not God’s idea. He doesn’t have two standards of morals, and I think the  time is coming when men will be glad to live up to the highest level of purity.”

“Don’t you think it seems worse for girls to swear or drink or gamble than for boys?”

“It does seem worse, because we have had such high ideals for women; but to God it must seem no worse, because he judges of us as souls, not as men and women, and He has laid down only one rule of conduct for all souls.”

"I'd like to know how the idea ever grew that it was not so bad for men to do wrong as for women."

"Perhaps we cannot now see all the reasons for this state of things, but we can see at least one reason. Many, many years ago men bought their wives, or took them by force from others, so they felt that they owned their wives. Of course, each man liked to feel that his wife was above reproach, that she really did belong to him; therefore, he held any lack of fidelity as a great sin against himself. But he did not think that he belonged to her. She had neither bought nor captured him, so she had no power over him, except such as she could gain by her fascinations.

"Naturally, he didn't care to be bound by the same rigid ideas to which he held her. He felt himself free to do what fancy dictated. The general level of morals was low, so he followed the pleasures of sense, and the wife could only submit, or try to be more fascinating to him than any one else. But if he was great and influential  or handsome, and was not bound by any moral restraints, there would be other women desirous of gaining his attentions and the material comforts he might be able to give, and he would quite willingly think himself free to follow his fancy without censure. In this way has grown up the double moral standard, the pure woman holding herself to the strictest morality, and men imagining themselves not so sternly held to the narrow path of absolute purity.

"Women are not now slaves, bought as wives and valued for their personal charms alone. They have intellectual power and moral force and social influence, and they can, if they will, create the single moral standard,  that is, the one high ideal for both men and women."

"O, father, do you think girls have as much power as that? It always seems to me as if girls might be of value when they are grown up, but that while we are girls we can't do much to make the world better."

"That is the mistake girls generally make, when in fact the most important time of life is youth. It is while you are girls that you are forming your own character, and at the same time you are helping to form the character of the generations to come. You are of far more value to the nation now, while you are young and can make of yourselves almost anything you please, than you will be when you are old and your habits are fixed. If girls all lived nobly and exacted noble conduct  of all their associates, boys as well as girls, it would not take long to settle all questions of reform. Young men will be what young women ask them to be, and that, you see, makes girls of great importance. Do you remember what we were reading in Sesame and Lilies the other day about woman's queenly power? Get the book and let us read it again."

Helen brought the book, and, finding the place, read:

"Woman's power is for rule, not for battle, and her intellect is not for invention or creation, but for sweet ordering, arrangement and decision. Her great function is Praise.

"There is not a war in the world, no, nor an injustice, but you women are answerable for it, not in that you have provoked, but in that you have not hindered. Men, by their nature, are prone to fight. They will fight for any cause or none. It is for you to choose their cause for them, and to forbid when there is no cause. There is no suffering, no injustice, no misery in the earth, but the guilt of it lies with you.

"Queens you must always be: queens to your lovers: queens to your husbands and sons: queens of higher mystery to the world beyond, which bows itself and will forever bow before the myrtle crown and the stainless sceptre of womanhood."

Helen leaned her head on her father's shoulder  in silence. Then she said, softly: "It makes me almost afraid to become a woman."

Mr. Wayne kissed his daughter tenderly, saying: "It is worthy your highest ambition to be a noble woman. I would be glad to see you such an one as is pictured in Lowell's poem of Irene. Would you like to read it to me?"

Helen took the book from her father's hand and read.

## IRENE.

Hers is a spirit deep, and crystal-clear;

Calmly beneath her earnest face it lies,

Free without boldness, meek without a fear,

Quicker to look than speak its sympathies;

Far down into her large and patient eyes

I gaze, deep-drinking of the infinite,

As, in the mid-watch of a clear, still night,

I look into the fathomless blue skies.

So circled lives she with Love's holy light,

That from the shade of self she walketh free:

The garden of her soul still keepeth she

An Eden where the snake did never enter;

She hath a natural, wise sincerity,

A simple truthfulness, and these have lent her

A dignity as moveless as the center:

So that no influence of earth can stir

Her steadfast courage, nor can take away

The holy peacefulness, which, night and day,

Unto her queenly soul doth minister.


Most gentle is she; her large charity

(An all unwitting, childlike gift to her)

Not freer is to give than meek to bear;

And, though herself not unacquaint with care,

Hath in her heart wide room for all that be—

Her heart that hath no secrets of its own,

But open as an eglantine full blown.

Cloudless forever is her brow serene,

Speaking calm hope and trust within her, whence

Welleth a noiseless spring of patience,

That keepeth all her life so fresh, so green

And full of holiness, that every look,

The greatness of her woman's soul revealing,

Unto me bringeth blessing, and a feeling

As when I read in God's own holy book.

A graciousness in giving that doth make

The small gift greatest, and a sense most meek

Of worthiness, that doth not fear to take

From others, but which always fears to speak

Its thanks in utterance, for the giver's sake;

The deep religion of a thankful heart,

Which rests instinctively in heaven's clear law

With a full peace, that never can depart

From its own steadfastness;—a holy awe

For holy things,—not those which men call holy,

But such as are revealed to the eyes

Of a true woman's soul bent down and lowly

Before the face of daily mysteries:

A love that blossoms soon, but ripens slowly

To the full goldenness of fruitful prime,


Enduring with a firmness that defies

All shallow tricks of circumstance and time,

By a sure insight knowing where to cling,

And where it clingeth never withering:

These are Irene's dowry, which no fate

Can shake from their serene, deep-builded state.

In-seeing sympathy is hers, which chasteneth
No less than loveth, scorning to be bound
With fear of blame, and yet which ever hasteneth
To pour the balm of kind looks on the wound,
If they be wounds which such sweet teaching makes,
Giving itself a pang for others' sakes:
No want of faith, that chills with sidelong eye,
Hath she; no jealousy, no Levite pride
That passeth by upon the other side:
For in her soul there never dwelt a lie.
Right from the hand of God her spirit came
Unstained, and she hath ne'er forgotten whence
It came, nor wandered far from thence,
But labored to keep her still the same,
Near to her place of birth, that she may not
Soil her white raiment with an earthly spot.
Yet sets she not her soul so steadily
Above, that she forgets her ties to earth,
But her whole thought would almost seem to be
How to make glad one lowly human hearth;
And to make earth next heaven; and her heart

Herein doth show its most exceeding worth,
That, bearing in our frailty her just part,
She hath not shrunk from evils of this life,
But hath gone calmly forth into the strife,
And all its sin and sorrows hath withstood
With lofty strength of patient womanhood:
For this I love her great soul more than all,

That, being bound, like us, with earthy thrall,

For with a gentle courage she doth strive

In thought and word and feeling so to live.

She walks so bright and heaven-like therein,—

Too wise, too meek, too womanly, to sin.

Like a lone star through riven storm-clouds seen

By sailors, tempest-tost upon the sea,

Telling of rest and peaceful havens nigh,

Unto my soul her star-like soul hath been,

Her sight as full of hope and calm to me;

For she unto herself hath builded high

A home serene, wherein to lay her head,

Earth's noblest thing, a Woman perfected.

"That is a beautiful picture of what a girl may be, and I'd be glad to see you making it your model."

"Yes," said Helen, slowly. Then, with more enthusiasm, "You know, father, I've always wished I were a boy. It seems so much grander to be a man than a woman. A man's life is so much freer, and he can do so much greater things, you know. Of course, I shall try to be a good woman,  but I wish women could do big things, the way men can."

"What wondrous things can men do that women can't do?" asked Mr. Wayne with a smile.

"Oh," replied Helen, clasping her hands with enthusiasm, "just see what men do. They build immense houses, and great bridges—Oh, they make the world, and women just sit in the house and look on. I'd like to do something."

Mr. Wayne smoothed back the hair from the forehead of his enthusiastic daughter with a tender smile, as he replied, "It does seem on the surface as if men did greater things than women, but it is only seeming, my dear. It is just as grand a thing to be a woman as to be a man. True, woman's work does not show on the surface so plainly, but she works with more enduring material than does man in creating the world of things. We can see the great works of man's hands and they impress us with a sense of his power; but it is mind that does the real work, and women have minds, or are minds, you know."

"Yes, I know, but they must devote their minds to cooking and dishwashing."

"I have seen women doing other things. In the old world I saw women digging ditches, carrying brick and mortar to the top of high buildings, ploughing in the fields; in fact, working just like men. The great buildings of the World's Exposition erected in Vienna in , were largely the work of women's hands. You are not anxious  to exchange dishwashing for such work, are you?"

"O, no, indeed; but it is man who plans such work and superintends its doing. A woman could not have planned Brooklyn bridge, for example."

"It is quite true that a woman did not plan it, but did you know that it was completed under a woman's supervision?"

"No, was it? How did that happen? Tell me all about it."

"It happened this way. Mr. Roebling, who was superintending its construction, was taken ill, and his wife took his place and personally gave oversight to every part of the work until it was done. You see, her being a woman did not prevent her doing the work. But if she had been only a careless or an ignorant woman she could not have done it. It was mind, you see, and cultured mind at that, which was the master power. If she had not been working with him in making the plans, she could not have worked for him in carrying them out. Instead of lamenting over your sex, you would better rejoice in the fact that you are a spirit, and realize that your power in all spheres of activity will be measured by the cultivation of your mental and spiritual powers."

"But, father, even if I do cultivate my mind, I shall probably never have an opportunity to do such a grand thing as help to build a Brooklyn bridge."

"Probably not, but you can do a greater thing.  You can fit yourself to work on finer material than insensate stones. You can mould plastic minds. It is a far greater thing to wield spiritual forces than to manipulate inorganic matter."

"But, all men do not merely make things. There are great statesmen, great soldiers, great writers."

"True, but you would not want to be a soldier, I am sure. To kill is not a glorious profession. And to be a great statesman or writer is not merely a question of sex; it is a question of mind."

"Do you think women have as much ability as men? Aren't men really smarter than women?"

Mr. Wayne smiled at the girl's eagerness. "I do not compare men and women to decide their relative ability," he answered. "I believe their minds differ, but that does not imply that one is superior and the other inferior. Each is superior in its own place."

"But men's minds are so much stronger, father. Women never can be on the same level as men."

"Bring me two needles of different sizes from your work basket. Now, tell me, which is superior to the other."

"That depends on what you want to do with them," replied Helen. "If you were going to sew on shoe buttons, you'd use this big one. If you wanted to hem a cambric handkerchief, you'd take this fine one."

"Just so. Each is superior in its special place, and both are necessary. This is just as it seems  to me in regard to the ability of men and women. They are both minds; one strong, robust, enduring rough usage; the other fine, delicate, going where the first cannot go, and therefore supplementing it, and increasing the range of work that can be accomplished. The fine needle might complain that it could not do hard work, but do you think the complaint would be justifiable?"

"Why, no, I don't; but tell me what great things a woman can do—things that are worth while, I mean; something besides keep house and take care of children. It seems to me that merely to be a cook and nurse girl is not a very high calling."

"She might be a chemist," suggested Mr. Wayne.

"Oh, yes, a few women might; but I mean something that I could be, or other girls like me who have no special talent."

"There is a great need of scientific knowledge among women. Every housekeeper needs to know something of chemistry. The woman who knows the chemical action of acids and alkalies on each other will never use soda with sweet milk, nor make the mistake of using an excess of soda with sour milk. And every day, in a myriad of ways, her knowledge of chemistry will be called into use."

"Then every woman should be a psychologist, most especially if she is to have the care of children."

"O, father, you use such big words. Tell me just what you mean."

"I mean that the office of nurse or mother demands the highest study of mental evolution. More big words, but I'll try to make you understand.

"It seems to you that any one can take care of a baby. But what is a baby? Not just a helpless little animal, to be fed and clothed and kept warm. A baby is a spirit in the process of development. From the moment of birth it is being educated by everything around it; the very tones of voice used in speaking to it are educating it. It is a great thing to be President of the United States, but that president was once a baby. His life depended on the way he was fed and cared for; his character was largely created by the circumstances of his life; and his mental powers—which he inherited from both parents—were in his babyhood and early childhood largely under the training of some woman. That woman, whether mother or nurse, had the first chance to develop him, to make him worthy or unworthy. John Quincy Adams said, 'All I am I owe to my mother,' and that is the testimony of many of earth's greatest men. Garfield's first kiss after his inauguration was very justly given to his mother.

"God has entrusted mothers with life's grandest work, the moulding of humanity in its plastic stage. You have done clay modelling in school, and you know that when the clay is fresh and  moist you can make of it almost anything you will, but when it has hardened it is past remodelling. It is just the same with humanity. In babyhood the mind is plastic; when one has grown to maturity, it is hard and unyielding. Man makes things; woman makes men. Which is the greater work?"

Helen hesitated. "It seems very noble as you talk of it, to train a child; but you know people don't feel that way. Mothers cuddle their babies, to be sure, but men think caring for babies is beneath them. They sneer at it as woman's work."

"Not all men, dear. Some of the great men of the world have spent years in the study of infancy, realizing that to know how the baby develops will enable them to understand better how to train it, and rightly to train babies is in reality to make the nation."

Helen, leaning her head back on her father's shoulder, was silent for a while, then she kissed him softly, saying, "Thank you, father dear. It has been a beautiful talk together. I am sure it will help me to be a better woman."

## CHAPTER II.

“Well, daughter,” said Mr. Wayne, as Helen and he were sitting by the fire one Sabbath afternoon while Mrs. Wayne had gone to her room to rest.

“Why,—” said Helen hesitatingly, “there is something I have been thinking about, but I’m afraid you’ll think it silly to ask you about it. You’ll think I ought to be able to decide it for myself.”

“Nothing that is of enough importance to be a problem to my daughter is silly to me. State your difficulty, and we’ll see if we cannot clear it away.”

“Well, father, I’d like to know what you think about boys and girls writing to each other. Of course, I don’t mean the foolish notes they send back and forth in school. I know that is silly, but I mean correspond. You see, Paul Winslow and Robert Bates are going to move away and they’re asking the girls to correspond with them, and the girls all say it will be great fun; but I don’t know. You know, mother has taught me that things that seem funny at one time don’t seem so at another, and I’ve been wondering if this is one of those things. When Robert asked me if I’d write to him I said I’d ask mother, and he seemed to get mad. He said if it was such a  dangerous thing to correspond with him that I had to ask my mother, he guessed I’d better not write to him. I said I asked my mother about everything. And he said ‘I suppose you show her your letters,’ and I said ‘Of course,’ and then he said he’d excuse me from writing to him. The girls all said I was very foolish; that it was perfectly right to correspond with boys you knew, and that our mothers wouldn’t want to be bothered to read all the letters we received. But I know mother doesn’t think it a bother, and I wouldn’t enjoy my letters if I didn’t share them with her.”

“You are certainly much safer to keep in confidence with your mother,” said Mr. Wayne, “and I should say that a young man who didn’t want you to show his letters to your mother is one you wouldn’t want to correspond with. I should be afraid that he’d be one who would show your letters to his boy friends and perhaps make fun of them.”

“O, father! Do you think that? It seems to me that wouldn’t be honorable.”

“Boys do not always have the highest ideals of honor, my dear. I remember once, when I was young, I was camping with a lot of young fellows. I think all of them were corresponding with girls, and these letters were common property. They were read aloud as we gathered around the camp fire in the evening; their bad spelling was laughed at and their silly sentimentalities  talked of in ways that I am sure would have made the girls’ cheeks burn with shame. They thought, of course, that the boy they wrote to would keep their letters as sweet secrets. I learned a good deal that summer about girls whom I had never seen. Some of them I came to know afterwards, and I often wondered what they would say if I should quote from their letters some foolish sentimentality which they imagined no one knew about except the one to whom it was written.”

“Then, father, you’d say we ought never to correspond with boys?”

“No, I didn’t quite say that. I can see that a friendly correspondence might be helpful. It seems to me that girls and boys can be a great help and inspiration to each other. I once had a girl correspondent who wrote most charming letters, simple recitals of her daily life with some of her little moralizings thrown in. Perhaps I would smile at them now, but they surely helped me to have higher ideals and made me have a great reverence for womanhood. There was one thing about her letters that I thought strange then, but I now think it very wise. She always signed every letter with her full name, never with her home pet name. I have often thought of it, and I believe it is a good plan. Certainly, if you knew that you would sign your full name to every letter, you would not be as apt to write foolishly as if your identity would be hidden under some nickname. And you never know what will become of your letters. A few days ago I read in the newspaper some foolish letters written by a girl to a man. She never imagined that any one else would read them. Yet here they were, in print, and the whole country was commenting on them. They were all signed by some soubriquet such as ‘Your darlingest Babe,’ or ‘Little Jimmy,’ and under the shield of such a signature she no doubt felt safe. But a dark tragedy tore away the flimsy protection and every one saw all her foolishness and sin.”

Helen shuddered. “I believe I’ll make it a rule,” she said, soberly, “to write only such things in my letters that I’d be willing to have printed over my own name.”

“That’s a good resolution, and I hope you’ll keep it. You can feel quite certain that if you don’t want to sign your own name to your letter you’d better not write it.

“There are a number of suggestions I would like to make to you along the line of your association with young men,” said Mr. Wayne, after a pause. “You have had no experience as yet, but in a few years you will be a woman and maybe then you’ll have no father or mother to give you counsel. As you know, I don’t want to shut you away from the society of young men, but I want you to know how to make it of the greatest advantage to you and to them.

“Do you know, dear, that women and girls  always make the moral standards which maintain in the society of which they form a part?”

Helen shook her head doubtfully. "I don't see how that can be," she said, "for everybody says that women are better than men; and I am sure boys do lots of things that we girls would never think of doing."

"Very true," replied Mr. Wayne, "but that is because the men and boys set higher standards for the women and girls than they in turn set for the men and boys. No boy would be seen in the street with a girl who was smoking a cigar; yet girls, good girls too, let boys smoke in their company. No matter how immoral a man may be, he always demands that the women who belong to him, his wife, mother, sister or sweetheart, shall be pure and above reproach. He will even claim that a wife's misconduct sullies his honor; but she never claims that his immorality is her responsibility. She will even marry a man whom she knows to be dissipated, foolishly trusting that her love will reform him. A broken heart and degenerate children too often prove how seriously she has failed. Yes, dear, I am right in saying that women are to blame that men do not have higher ideals and live up to them. Ruskin says, 'The soul's armor is never well set to a heart unless a woman's hand has braced it; and it is only when she braces it loosely that the honor of manhood fails.'"

"It's putting a great responsibility on women, isn't it?" sighed Helen.

"Yes, daughter, but no greater than is placed on man. Each sex should be the protector and inspirer of the other. But instead of that, they often tempt and mislead each other."

"Good girls don't tempt boys, father."

"I'm afraid that they do, dear. They may not be aware of what they are doing, but nevertheless they may be sources of temptation."

"I really don't see how."

"Probably not, but I can tell you, for I remember my own youth and know how girls may tempt boys unwittingly. When in college I was a boarder in a family where there were several other students, and two or three pretty High School girls. One of them was very coquettish, and was always 'making goo-goo eyes,' at the boys, as they say now-a-days. She couldn't talk in a straightforward manner, but always with sidewise glances from downcast lids that seemed invitations to a nearer approach.

"Among the students was one who was very retiring and bashful. He rarely spoke to the girls and seemed quite embarrassed if they spoke to him. This girl seemed to set herself to work to flirt with him. She would glance up at him so appealingly that we boys couldn't help guying him about it. One evening when she was plying her arts—not with evil intent, but she loved to flirt and did not understand  what that might mean to a young man—all at once he seized her around the waist and kissed her furiously. She was in a rage in a moment, and said some pretty sharp things about his lack of gentlemanliness.

"He stood his ground without flinching. 'I'm as much of a gentleman as you are a lady,' he said. 'I have let you alone, but you have been tormenting me for weeks. You liked to try how far you could go, and thought yourself virtuous because you felt no temptation. You didn't care how you tempted me, or the other boys. You have tried your powers in public. O, yes, you are too good to be sly! And so I determined to give you a public lesson, and everybody here, I am sure, is thankful to me for it. Now, perhaps, you will let us alone. We want to be good, we want to treat all women with respect; yet, when you pretty pink-and-white creatures smile and smirk and set us on fire, then you say we are bad, we are not gentlemen. Maybe not. But we are men, and we should find in you the true womanhood which is our salvation.'

"I can see him now, as he stood up so proudly, forgetting his bashfulness in his righteous indignation,—and we all applauded him, I am glad to say. The girl was offended with us all, and left the house and sought another boarding place. In her stead came a real, true, womanly girl. Full of fun, a real comrade, ready to join our sports, to help us in every way possible, but  always making us feel that we were in honor bound to protect her from even a flirtatious thought. Every man in the house was her friend, some of them, I am sure, her adorers, but none ever ventured to approach her with familiarity. If she should meet any of us to-day, she would not have to blush in the presence of her husband and children at the memory of any happening of those days.

"This is the kind of a woman I want you to be, my daughter dear, a woman realizing a woman's true place and power, as Ruskin says, 'Power to heal, to redeem, to guide, to guard!' Just hand me the book and let me read you a few words from his essay on War. 'Believe me!' he says, 'the whole course and character of your lovers' lives is in your hand. What you would have them be they shall be, if you not only desire but deserve to have them so; for they are but mirrors in which you will see yourselves imaged. If you are frivolous, they will be so also; if you have no understanding of the scope of their duty, they will also forget it; they will listen,—they can listen—to no other interpretation of it than that uttered from your lips. Bid them be brave;—they will be brave for you; bid them be cowards, and how noble soever they be, they will quail for you. Bid them be wise, and they will be wise for you; mock at their counsels and they will be fools for you, such, and so absolute is your rule over them.' Isn't  that a wonderful power that is in woman's hands? And it is true, as he further says, just here: 'Whatever of the best he can conceive, it is her part to be; whatever of the highest he can hope, it is hers to promise; all that is dark in him she must purge into purity; all that is failing in him she must strengthen into truth; from her, through all the world's clamour, he must win his praise; in her, through all the world's warfare, he must find his peace.'"

Helen sighed. "It is so much to ask," she said. "Has nothing been written to the men, how they must help and protect women?"

Mr. Wayne smiled, as he kissed his little daughter and said, "Whatever has been written for men I will keep to tell my son, and I trust it will help him to reverence all womanhood."

## CHAPTER III.

As Mrs. Wayne and her daughter sat at their window they saw a carriage dash by containing a handsomely dressed woman. Shortly after a very pretty girl passed the house, talking busily with a boy of her own age.

"How funny some mothers are," said Helen. "That was Mrs. Eversman who rode by just now, and that's Corrinne, her daughter. Mrs. Eversman pays no attention to Corrinne except to buy her pretty clothes, and scold her for carelessness. Corrinne goes where she pleases. She has lots of beaux, and when they call she won't let her mother come into the parlor,—she says she doesn't want her 'snooping' around, and Mrs. Eversman only laughs. She seems to think it smart. And, mother, Corrinne has such lovely presents from boys and young men. And when she goes to the theatre with a young man, she insists on having a carriage and flowers and a supper afterward. She says no fellow need come around her unless he has 'the spondulics,' she calls money."

"Poor child!" said Mrs. Wayne thoughtfully. "How little she understands the purpose of life!"

"But she says she wants to have a good time," urged Helen.

"Surely," was Mrs. Wayne's reply. "Every  girl is entitled to a good time, but that does not of necessity consist of spending money. I should think she wouldn't like to be under such obligations to young men."

"O, I guess she doesn't think she is under obligations. She thinks they are under obligation to her for condescending to go with them. But, mother, ought a girl let a young man spend money on her?"

"I hope, my dear, when you are old enough to go out with young men that you will care too much for yourself to be willing to take expensive gifts. A certain amount of expenditure is allowable. A few flowers, a book, or a piece of music, but never elegant jewelry or articles of clothing. That is not only bad taste but it is often a direct incentive for young men of small salaries to be dishonest. Corrinne, and girls like her, do not know how much they may be responsible for young men becoming untrue to their business trusts, nor how much they might do to strengthen young men in their purposes to be honest. You remember Aunt Elsie and Uncle Harold. He is a man of means now, but he was once a poor young clerk. He admired Elsie and wanted to show her every attention, but she knew his salary would not permit extravagance; so when he first asked her to go to some public entertainment, he said he would come with a carriage at the appointed time. At once she said decidedly, 'Then I will not go. It is not far.  If it is a fine night, we can walk. If it rains, we can go on the street cars. You may send me a few flowers, but we will not have an opera supper nor indulge in needless carriages!' Of course he objected, and urged that he could afford it. 'But I can't,' was her reply. And years after, when they were married, he confessed that it was a great relief to him to be able to take her about in ways that suited his purse and yet have no fear of being thought mean. Now he can buy her everything her heart can desire; but he acknowledges that he might not have been able to withstand the temptation had she in her younger days desired pleasures beyond his power honorably to provide."

"Mother," said Helen after a pause, as two girls passed the house with their arms about each other's waists. "Don't you think it silly for girls to be so 'spooney'?"

"I certainly think it is in bad taste for them to be so publicly demonstrative, and I could wish that girls might be friends with each other more as boys are. Now, there are Paul and Winfield. Surely no girls ever thought more of each other than these two boys, and yet I fancy we would smile to see them embracing each other on all occasions, as Lucy and Nellie do."

"I should say so! I've heard Paul say, 'Old Chap,' or seen Winfield give Paul a slap on the shoulder; but they are never silly and they've been friends for years. But Lucy and Nellie  have only been so 'thick' for a few weeks, and they'll fall out pretty soon. Lucy is always having such lover-like friends and then quarreling with them. Now, she and Nellie are going to have a mock wedding next week. They call themselves husband and wife even now,—isn't that silly?"

"It is worse than silly,—I call it wrong," replied Mrs. Wayne. "Such morbid friendships are dangerous, both to health and morals."

"To the health, mother? I don't see how that can be."

"No, I doubt if you can, but I hope that you will believe me when I tell you they are dangerous. When girls are so demonstrative, when they claim to stand to each other as man and woman, you may feel assured that the relation is unnatural and that the drain upon the nervous system is very great. I once knew a girl who actually destroyed the health of a number of girls in a school by such demonstrative friendships. She always had one devoted friend who could not live without her. I have known a girl to cry day after day and actually go home sick, because her friendship with this girl was threatened. And it is said that another girl took her own life from jealousy of this one.

"Friendship is a grand thing when it is true and worthy, but a morbid, unnatural sentimentality does not deserve the name of friendship and I should be very sorry to see you fall into the toils of a morbid, unnatural relation with another  girl. Yet I should be pleased to see you having a sincere, womanly, noble affection for another girl, one which would not waste itself in sentimentality but be able to rise to heights of grand renunciation."

"I think I understand you, mother, and I promise you I will try to hold the highest ideals of friendship."

Such talks as these brought mother and daughter into such close companionship that Helen was not afraid to bring her mother the deepest problems of her young life.

It was Saturday afternoon, and mother and daughter were sitting together sewing. The rain was pouring, so that there was little fear of visitors, and while Mrs. Wayne was discussing with herself how she could begin to talk to her daughter of her approaching womanhood, Helen suddenly said, "Mother, what is the matter with Clara Downs? She is going into consumption, they say, and I heard Sadie Barker say to Cora Lee that it was because Clara did not change into a woman. What did she mean? I thought we just grew into women. Isn't that the way?"

"You didn't ask Sadie what she meant?"

"O, no, the girls acted as if they didn't want me to hear, and then, I'd always rather you'd tell me things, for then I feel sure that I know them right."

This little testimony of her trust in her mother furnished Mrs. Wayne with the desired opportunity,  and she said, "In order that you may clearly understand Sadie's remark I shall have to make a long explanation of how girls become women."

"Why, mother, don't we just grow into women?"

"Well, my dear, I shall have to say both yes and no to that question. Girls do grow and become women, but women are something more than grown-up girls. This house is much bigger than it was two years ago. Did it just grow bigger?"

"Why, no, not exactly. There are no more rooms now than there were before, but some rooms have been finished off and are used now, when before they weren't used at all, and so the house seems bigger. But it can't be that way with our bodies, for we don't have any new organs added or finished off to make us women?"

"That is just what is done, my daughter."

"What! New organs added, mother? What can you mean?"

"I mean, dear, that your bodily dwelling is enlarged, not by the addition of new rooms, but by the completing of rooms that have as yet not been fitted up for use."

"I don't understand you, mother."

"I suppose not, but I hope to be able to make you understand. You have studied your bodily house and know of the rooms in the different stories, the kitchen, laundry, dining-room, picture-gallery and telegraph office,—in fact, all the rooms or organs that keep you alive; but there is one part of the house that you have not studied. There are various rooms or organs which are not needed to keep you alive, and which have, therefore, been closed. As you approach womanhood, these organs will wake up and become active, and their activity is what will make you a woman."

"Why, mother, it sounds like a fairy story, a tale of a wonderful magic palace, doesn't it? And Clara Downs hasn't got these marvelous rooms?"

"Yes, they are there, but they are evidently not being finished off for use. I think, however, the girls made the mistake of confounding cause and effect. They say she is going into consumption because she does not become a woman. I think she does not become a woman because she is going into consumption. Do you know why we did not finish off these rooms in our house sooner?"

"Why, father said he had not the money."

"That is right. He did not say that he did not have the money because he did not finish off the rooms."

"My, no, that would have been absurd; but I don't see how that applies to Clara?"

"It needed money to finish off our house; so it needs vitality to change from girl to woman, and Clara seems not to have the vitality. She is failing in health, hence she has not vital force  to spend in completing her physical development."

"But, mother, tell me more about this wonderful change. Where are the new rooms and what is their purpose? I can't really believe that I have some bodily organs that I never heard of. What are they and where are they; when will they be finished off? I am all curiosity. Didn't we study about them in our school physiology?"

"You have given me a good many questions to answer, little girl, and I hardly know where to begin answering them.

"In your school physiology you studied all about the organs that keep you alive. What did you learn about your bodily house? How many stories is it?"

"Three stories high, and then there is a cupola on the top of all. I like to think of the head as a cupola or observatory, resting on the tower of the neck and turning from side to side as we want to look around us."

"And what is the furniture in the different stories?"

"O, the upper story is called the thorax, and the one big room in it is the thoracic cavity. It contains the heart and lungs. The next story below is the abdominal cavity and it has a number of articles of furniture, the liver, the stomach, the spleen, the bowels, etc. Then the lower story is—O, I've forgotten what it is called."

"The lower story is called the pelvis."

"O, yes, and the pelvic cavity contains the reservoirs for waste material. I remember you told me that once."

"That is right. The pelvic cavity contains the bladder, which is the reservoir for waste fluid, and the rectum, the outlet for waste solids. But it contains more than these. It is here in the pelvis that these organs of which you have not heard are located. You remember when you asked me about yourself and how you came into the world I told you of a little room in mother's body where you lived and grew until you were large enough to live your own independent existence. Did you ever wonder where this room is?"

"Why, I never thought much about it. I guess I just thought it was in the abdominal cavity. Isn't it?"

"No, the room is a little sac that lies here in the pelvis. I can best explain it to you by a picture. Here it is. You see it looks like a  pear hanging with the small end down. It lies just between the bladder and the rectum, and a passage leads up to it."

"O, I see. Doesn't the bladder empty itself through that passage?"

"No, the outlet to the bladder is just at the very entrance to this passage, but does not open into the passage at all. This passage is called the vagina, and the little room has two names. One is Latin, uterus; the other is Saxon, womb—it means the place where things are brought to life. The Latin word is used by scientists, but the Saxon word is used in the Bible and by poets. Do you remember when Nicodemus came to Jesus that he was told he must be born again, and he said in surprise, 'Can a man enter the second time into his mother's womb and be born?'"

"O, I see now what he meant. I could not understand it before. Of course, he knew that was impossible, and so he could not see what Jesus meant."

"David says, 'Thou hast covered me in my mother's womb. I will praise thee, for I am fearfully and wonderfully made.' Poets sometimes speak of the womb of the morning, meaning the place where morning lies and grows until it is ready to burst forth in beauty on the world."

"I like the Saxon word better than the Latin one, don't you?"

"Yes, but as scientists use the Latin word we  shall use that, so that we will know how to talk on these subjects scientifically. The uterus hangs suspended by two broad ligaments (marked ll in the picture). There are also round ligaments from the back and front which hold it loosely in place. On the back of each broad ligament is an oval body called the ovary (marked o).

"Do you remember once seeing in a hen that Ellen was preparing for dinner a great number of eggs of all sizes? That was the hen's ovary. Ovum means an egg, and ovary means the place of the eggs."

"O, mother, women don't have eggs, do they? I don't like that."

"Well, if you do not like to use the word egg we can say ovum, which, you know, is the Latin word for egg. The plural is ova. Or we may call the ovum the germ, which means the primary source. The ovum or germ is a very tiny thing, so small that it cannot be seen without a microscope;  laid side by side would make only one inch in length."

"O, mother, that is wonderful."

"Yes, dear. The whole process of life is very wonderful and very beautiful. The uterus and ovaries belong to what is called the reproductive system. As I said, until now your vital forces have been employed in keeping you alive. Your nutritive system, your muscular system, your nervous system and so on, have all been busy taking  care of you only; but soon your reproductive system will awaken and begin to take on activity."

"And what does that mean, mother?"

 "It means that you are entering on what is known as the maternal period of your life; are actually becoming a woman with all a woman's power of becoming a mother."

"But you don't mean that a girl of fourteen could become a mother?"

"Yes, it might be possible; but no girl of fourteen should be a mother, for she is not fully developed and her children will not be strong as if she had not married until after she were twenty."

"But tell me, mother, all about it. I don't see now how the baby grows?"

"Well, I was showing you the ovary in which are many ova. As the girl nears the age of fourteen, these ova start to grow and once a month one ripens and is thrown out of the ovary. It is taken up by the Fallopian tube, marked od  in the picture, and it passes down the tube into the uterus and through the vagina out into the world."

"Can one tell when it passes?"

"No, but there is a sign that this change has taken place. The uterus is lined with a membrane in which are many blood vessels, and when the girl has reached this stage of development and becomes a woman, the vessels become very full of blood, so full that it oozes out through the walls of the blood vessels into the cavity of the uterus, and when it passes out of the vagina the girl becomes aware of it and knows that she has become a woman.

"This process takes place once a month and is called menstruation, from the Latin mensum, a month."

"Isn't it painful, mother?"

"It ought not to be and is not, if the girl is perfectly well. But sometimes girls have dressed improperly and have displaced their internal organs, or they have exhausted themselves with pleasure-seeking, or in some other way have injured themselves, in which case they may suffer much pain. When girls get about this age mothers are very anxious about them, very desirous that they shall naturally and easily step over into the land of womanhood."

"I should think that girls ought to be taught about themselves, so that they would not do the things which injure them."

"I think they should, and that is why I am telling you all this to-day so that when the change comes to you, you will not be frightened and maybe do something from which you will suffer all your life long, as many girls have done.

"The question of tight clothing becomes now much more important than ever before. You can see at once that the restriction of the clothing comes just over the part of the body where there is the least resistance."

"Oh, yes, I remember about the seven upper ribs, that are fastened to both spine and breast-bone; and the five lower ribs, that are fastened directly only to the spine and are attached in front to the breast-bone by cartilage; and the two floating ribs, lowest of all, and fastened only to the spine. I have often wondered why the important organs of the abdominal cavity should not have been better protected.”

“It was needful to leave the front of the body covered only with muscular structure, or it could not be bent and twisted about as we can now bend it, and that would have hindered our activity. Just imagine yourself going about encased in bone from your shoulders to your hips.”

Helen laughed merrily. “I shouldn’t like it,” she said, “but that is just what is done by the corset, and folks get used to that.”

“Yes, they become accustomed to the pressure because the nerves lose their sensitiveness and  no longer report their discomfort to the brain; but the injury continues, nevertheless.”

“Mother, I wish you’d tell me just how tight clothing is injurious. So many of the girls laugh at me because I don’t wear a corset, and they declare it does not hurt them. They all say they wear their clothes perfectly loose and they think they prove it by showing me how they can run their fists up under their dress waists.”

“Certainly, that can be done even with a very tight dress, by just pressing a little more air out of the lungs; but that is not a true measurement. To learn if the dress is tight, one should unfasten all of the clothing, draw in the breath slowly until the lungs are filled to their utmost capacity. Then, while the lungs are held full, see if the clothing can be fastened without allowing any air to escape. If it can, then it is not tight; but if the lungs must be compressed, ever so little, in order to allow the clothing to be fastened, it is too tight. You see, the power we have to breathe is the measure of our power to do, and to lessen our breathing capacity is to lessen our ability in all directions.

“I saw a statement yesterday that will interest you. It was a recital of an experiment made by Dr. Sargent on twelve girls in running  yards in  minutes  seconds. The first time they ran without corsets and their waists measured  inches. The pulse was counted before running and found to beat  times a minute. Again,  it was counted after running and found to have risen to . The second run was made in the same length of time, but with corsets on, which reduced the waist measure to  inches. Pulse before running ; after running , showing the extra effort the heart was obliged to make because of the restriction of the waist and consequent lessening of the breathing power. He also found that the corset reduced the breathing capacity one-fifth.

"Let me read you another little item:

"'Dr. Dickenson has been studying the pressure of the corset. He says that in the ordinary breathing we have to overcome in the resistance and elasticity of chest and lungs a force of  pounds. If the woman whose waist measure is  inches wears a corset of the same size, so that her waist is not compressed at all, there is added a force of  pounds. If her natural waist measure is  inches and is reduced by the corset to ½ inches, the pressure is  pounds.'

"When Dr. Lucy Hall was physician at Vassar College, she made some observations as to the mental powers manifested by those who wore and those who did not wear corsets. In a graduating class in which there were thirty-five girls, nineteen wore no corsets; eighteen members of the class took honors, and of these thirteen wore no corsets; seven of the class were appointed to take part in public on Commencement Day, and six of these wore no corsets. All who took  prizes for essays wore no corsets; five girls were class-day orators, and four of these wore no corsets; five had not missed a day in four years, and one had not missed a day in six years. That speaks pretty loudly in favor of doing without corsets, doesn't it?"

"Yes, indeed; but some of the girls care more for looks than for class honors. They say a girl looks so queer without a corset."

"That is because we have set up false standards of beauty. If we examine the finest statuary of all ages, we shall not find a single figure that has been accustomed to tight clothing. The artist copies God's ideal figure of the woman, not that of the fashion plate. You see, we have become so accustomed to the deformed figure that we call it beautiful, just as the Chinese woman thinks her deformed foot is beautiful."

"O, isn't it dreadful that the Chinese bind up the feet of the little girls as they do?"

"It certainly is; but not as dreadful as that Christian women bind up the vital parts of the body and prevent their working as they should. One can live without feet, but one could not live without heart and lungs and other vital organs, and can only half live when these organs are cramped and crowded together so they cannot work properly. If we were all truly artistic we would be pained at the sight of the small waist, for we should know that it was procured at the expense of the vital organs. You have heard of the statue  of the Venus de Medici, renowned as being the most beautiful representation of a woman's figure?"

"O, yes, I have seen pictures of it."

"A certain English actress was called a model of loveliness in form and feature. Some one has made a comparison between the two. Here are the pictures and measurements:

"You see how graceful the curves of the Venus how abrupt those of the actress and yet to most people her figure looks the more elegant. But I want to call your attention to the fact that to create her figure is really to lose much space, and to crowd together the important  vital organs until their working power is greatly hindered. This same actress has become enlightened and now says: 'Of course, no woman can breathe properly in a tightly-laced corset. I am horrified when I think of the way I used to compress my waist, and look back at the pictures showing my hour-glass figure with positive amazement.'

"Don't you think it strange that we never want little rooms with furniture huddled close together, except in our bodily dwellings? The Divine Architect has given us grand apartments, with all the machinery harmoniously related, and we think we improve things by putting everything into the closest possible quarters and disturbing the harmony! But the damage is not done to the heart and lungs alone. The liver is crowded out of place until it sometimes reaches clear across the abdomen and is creased with ruts from the pressure of the ribs upon it. The stomach is also pressed out of place. It belongs close up under the diaphragm, but it is crowded by the pressure down until it lies in the abdominal cavity, as low down, sometimes, as the umbilicus, six or eight inches below where it belongs."

"O, mother, that seems awful."

"It is awful, my dear, because the body is created to do certain work, and to do that work well, its laws should be regarded. We would not think of interfering with the works of a watch or a piano, because they are valuable, but we  do not hesitate to interfere with the more valuable organs of our bodies, and we do not even think that we are offering an insult to the Creator.

"But I have not told you yet of the evil effects in the displacement of the bowels. Do you remember how many feet of intestines there are in the body?"

"About twenty feet of small and about four feet of large intestines."

"And how are they held in place?"

"Why, I don't just remember."

"The small intestines are encased in a membrane called the mesentery. It is just as if I folded this strip of cloth in the middle lengthwise  and put my finger inside of the fold. The small intestines lie in the middle fold of the mesentery, and the edges of the mesentery are gathered up like a ruffle and fastened to the spine in a space of about six inches, leaving it to flare out like a very full ruffle. In this way, you see, the intestines are left free, and yet cannot tie themselves in knots as they might if but laid loosely in the abdominal cavity.

 "If the waist is constricted above them, they sink down and pull on this attachment, and that often causes backache and inability to stand or  walk with comfort. It may also press the reproductive organs out of place, and so cause much pain and suffering at menstruation.

"I am of the opinion that women were not intended to be invalids in any degree because of their womanhood; and very likely there would be much less flow at menstrual periods if women and girls lived in accordance with Nature's laws."

"But, mother, you have not told me what this blood is for. It seems as if it would not be necessary for women to go through such an experience every month."

"Perhaps we do not fully know why it should be so, but we do know when the little child is growing in its little room, the mother does not have the menstrual flow; so we may suppose that it goes to nourish the child."

"O, I see, and when not needed for the child, it just passes away."

"Yes, and every time this occurs it says to the woman that she is a perfect woman, capable of all the duties of the wife and mother. This thought should make her think very sacredly of herself."

For a few moments there was silence between mother and daughter, broken only by the sound of the falling rain. At length Helen spoke. "Mother, there is something I want to ask you about. You remember last summer, when Mrs. Vale and Mrs. Odell called on you, I was in the library and they did not see me. While they  were waiting for you they began to talk of Edith Chenowyth and of something dreadful she had been doing. They called her a very bad girl. When you came in they spoke to you about her and you said 'Poor child, I am sorry for her;' and they were quite angry that you should pity her. Just before they left I made some slight noise, and Mrs. Vale said, 'I hope no one heard what we've said,' and you said, 'I hope not, I am sure.' So I thought you would not want me to know of it or I should have asked you about what it all meant.

"Yesterday I heard some of the girls talking and one said, 'Did you know that Edith Chenowyth had a baby last night? She is down at old Mrs. Fein's. Her folks have turned her out of the house.' Then Clara Downs said, 'Well, they ought to turn her out, acting as she has.' Then they all said such dreadful things of her! And while they were talking, Cora Lee came up and said, 'O, girls, I am an Auntie! My sister Ada had the loveliest baby boy last night and my father gave her $ because it is his first grandson; and the baby's father opened a bank account in the name of Charles Wyndham Bell. Ada is just as happy as she can be and we are all so proud.'

"Now, mother, Ada Lee and Edith Chenowyth were in the same class at school; they sang a duet together on the day of their graduation and Edith was just as lovely as Ada. Now she has a  baby and every one scorns her, while Ada has one and she is honored and loved. I wish you'd explain this to me."

"Well, my daughter, you see Ada is married and Edith is not."

"Yes, I know that; and yet that does not explain to me why a child should be an honor to one and a disgrace to the other. I know people think so, but I want to know why."

"In order to make you understand why, I shall have to take you back to your lessons in botany. You recall how you learned there of the reproduction of plants. You learned that the pollen must pass down the style and fertilize the seed before it would grow; and you learned that the stamen, anther and pollen were the male part of the plant and the ovary, style and stigma the female part of the plant."

"Yes, and I remember that I thought it rather silly that in a school book the plants should be spoken of as people, as if it were a fairy story."

"And yet, my dear, it was only stating an actual fact, and was not, as you fancied, a fairy story. There are really fathers and mothers among plants; if there were not there could be no new plant life. In some plants the male and female are united in the same flower; in other plants there are male and female flowers, but all growing on the same plant. In a third species all the flowers of one plant will be male, and all of another plant will be female. The fertilization of plants is very interesting, for the insects and the bees and the breezes often carry the pollen of the male flowers to the female flowers, and so the seeds are fertilized.

"When we come to study reproduction among the human race, we find the same plan; in fact, we find it in all forms of organized life, plants, animals and man. That is, there must be fathers as well as mothers.

 "I told you of the germ or ovum that is produced by the ovary of the woman. That ovum of itself could never become a new being. It must be united with a life-giving principle furnished by the man. This principle consists of a fluid in which float tiny little creatures called spermatozoa—one is a spermatozoon. Here is a picture of some. They are too small to be seen without the aid of a microscope. They are about / of an inch long, that is,  of them laid end to end, would cover only an inch in length.

"If an ovum starts from the ovary and is not hindered, it will pass on through the uterus and the vagina into the world, and that is the end of it; but if, when the ovum starts from the ovary to make its way through the tube, the spermatozoa are deposited here at the mouth of the uterus, they will find their way up into the cavity, and if one meets an ovum and enters into it, a new life is begun. The ovum will now fasten itself to the walls of the uterus and grow into the little child.

"You can understand that, for the spermatozoa to be placed where they can find their way into the uterus, means a very close and familiar relation of the man and woman.

"When two people have decided that they love each other so well that they are willing to leave all friends and ties of home, and in the presence of witnesses promise to live together always, and a clergymen has conducted a solemn ceremony and pronounced them husband and wife, it is perfectly proper for them to do what before would not have been proper.

"They may go and live in a house by themselves, occupy the same room, bear the same name and be, in the eyes of the community, as one person.

"If they desire to call into life a little child of their own, it is fully in accordance with the laws of God and man, and no one can criticise them. They have violated no ideas of purity  or propriety. But you can understand that if an unmarried woman has a child, every one knows that she has had, with some man, an intimate relation to which they had no right, either moral or legal. They have sacrificed modesty and purity, and the child is a badge of disgrace, rather than of honor."

"Isn't it just as much of a disgrace to him as to her?"

"Yes, dear, I think it is, and so do many of the best people; but, unfortunately, there are many who do not think so, and blame the woman or girl altogether. And the man, very likely, does not blame himself. He says, 'Well, she ought not to have permitted it,' and so he gets out of the way and leaves her to bear the shame alone. It is a cowardly thing to do, for in all probability he was the one who made the first advances and, had she been wise, she would have shunned the man who tried to lead her into wrong, into doing that which would forfeit her self-respect and the respect of the world. Even the man scorns the woman whom he leads into disgrace."

"I suppose girls don't understand it, do they? Now, I did not understand, until just now as you have told me about it, and I believe lots of the girls are going into danger and don't know it. I must tell you something. Yesterday as I was walking home from school with Belle Dane—you know her, don't you? Isn't she pretty?"

"Yes, she is pretty, and I should imagine pert also. She has no mother."

"Well, as we were walking along, a young man passed us. Belle smiled and bowed, and he bowed too. I said, 'Who is that?' She said, 'I don't know, but isn't he handsome? I shouldn't wonder if he'd turn back and walk with us!' And sure enough, in a moment he was walking at her side, saying, 'What a lovely day? Do you walk here every day?' and she said, 'Yes, as I go from school. On Saturdays I walk by the lake.'

"'Ah,' he said, 'I am thinking of walking there to-morrow. At what hour do you walk?' 'About  o'clock,' she said. Then he looked at me. 'Does your friend walk there, too? I have a friend who'd be glad to come.' Then I broke in—'No, I never walk by the lake.' Then he bowed and left, and Belle said, 'O, you little goose! Why did you say you didn't walk by the lake? He'd have brought his friend and we'd have had such a good time. Ten to one he'll bring flowers or candy, and we could take a boat ride. You were foolish.' And I said, 'I don't want to walk with young men, especially if I don't know them.' And she laughed and said, 'O, you'll get over that when you're older and learn what fun it is. My, he's a gentleman! See how nice he dressed and what pretty teeth he had and what nice words he used.' Now, I thought maybe I was silly, but after what you have told me to-day, I think she is  going in dangerous places and maybe don't know it. I am so glad you told me."

"Yes, poor child! It was just so that Edith began. She met a handsome young man. She thought him a gentleman because he dressed fine. She let him hold her hand, then put his arm around her and kiss her, and so, little by little, he led her on, and she thought it was all so nice,—and now she is friendless and in great trouble."

"Mother, it makes me think of a little girl I saw at the seaside last summer. She was dancing on the edge of the waves. They came up and washed over her little pink toes and she laughed with delight. After a time the tide rose a little higher and the waves dashed over her feet and still she thought it fun; and then came one big wave and threw her down and carried her out to sea, and if there hadn't been some sailors right there with a boat she would have been drowned,—and all the time she thought it fun till the last wave came, and then she was frightened awfully."

"Your illustration is a very good one, my daughter, and I fear that poor Belle is dancing in the gentle foam of a wave that will grow in power till it carries her out to sea, a lost girl."

"Mother, I really don't see how a girl can let a man become so familiar with her. I should think it would disgust her at once; and yet Edith seemed like a perfect lady."

"No doubt you will understand this puzzling matter better after a few years than you do now,  but I can explain it to you partly. It is a part of human nature that men and women are very attractive to each other, and in a way that does not exist between men and men or women and women. It may be called a sort of personal magnetism. As they begin to develop into men and women, they begin to feel this new attraction. They want to please each other. New feelings and emotions are felt. If their hands touch, they feel a sort of electric thrill, even the glance of the eye may cause the same thrill. They enjoy it, and they do not know what it means. They do not know that, while it is pleasant, it is also dangerous.

"Girls are more ignorant than young men, because, as a rule, they have been taught less. The young men know more, but in all probability they have not learned from sources that are pure. The young girl does not understand that her coquettish glances and tossings of the head and simperings are so many intuitive efforts to awaken that sort of magnetic thrill in the young man. If she knew it, she would see that it is more maidenly to hold in check all actions that would tend to make the young man desire to be familiar with her."

"But, mother, if it is not right to be familiar, why does God make us with those desires?"

"God has given us many desires that are right under certain conditions and wrong under others and He has given us reason with which to control our desires. It is right to eat when the food  is our own, but wrong to eat if we have stolen the food. It is right to enjoy the attraction of one to whom our heart and life is given, but otherwise we are defrauding some one else. You can understand that you would not want the man you are to marry to have had familiarities with many other girls, neither would he like to think that other men had been permitted to be free with you.

"If you were going to select a dress that was to last all your life long, you would not choose goods that had been handled and were shop-worn. Even so with husband and wife. Each likes to feel sure that the freshest, purest love of the heart and modesty of person has been kept unstained from the slightest unwarrantable familiarity.”

## CHAPTER IV.

"O Mother, I am so glad you are at home again. I had a lovely talk with father last evening, but it wasn't you. He gave me lots to think about, though. He said that mothers need to have such a broad education; that they should even be chemists, mother, think of that!"

"Does that seem such a strange idea to you? Really they need to be much more than that. They should be good teachers, to instruct their children, wise judges, in order to know what justice is, doctors of medicine so as to understand the first symptoms of illness and how to treat it, and surgeons so as to know how to bind up wounds, treat cuts and bruises and even how to reduce a dislocated finger if necessary. They should be physiologists so as to understand the laws of bodily health, and psychologists so as to know and obey the laws of the mental development of their children."

"O, mother! How can one girl learn all those hard things?"

Mrs. Wayne smiled indulgently as she replied, "O, she won't have to learn all of them at once. Taken one at a time, through all the years preceding her marriage, she will find she can learn something of each without taxing herself too severely.  For example, you can learn now how to take care of your own health, and that will help you to care for the health of your children when they come. You have already studied First Aid to the injured in your physiology class. When you go to College you will study psychology as a part of your course of study."

"What does that big word mean, mother?"

"Psychology means the science of mind. I said that mothers need to be psychologists; that is, students of the science of mind, so that they will understand the indications of the development of mind in their babies. A child gets the largest part of its education before it is six years old."

"O, mamma, do you really mean that?"

"I certainly do. In the first place, it has to learn, one by one, and by repeated experiments, its body. You do not realize now that you had to learn, one by one, and by repeated experiments, every one of the muscular movements that you can now make without thinking of them. You remember what hard work it was to learn the piano and that was only learning to use a very few muscles in a certain way. As a baby you had to practice hours a day before you could learn to hold anything in your fingers. Your little hands flew about very wildly at first, but by constant practice you gained skill at last."

"Why, mamma, I never thought that a baby was practicing when it was throwing its hands about."

"But it is practicing, and it keeps it up hour  after hour, day after day, until it has learned to hold things, to pull itself up, to sit up, to hold its head up, to creep, to walk, to climb.

"Have you any idea what a wonderful feat has been accomplished when a baby has learned to walk? Physiologists tell us that walking is continually beginning to fall and perpetual recovery from falling. It is a greater thing for the baby than those acrobatic feats which so amazed you the other day.

"Then the mental education begins also at birth. The baby is building his brain by everything he sees and does, and it is the mother's duty to see that this brain-building goes on in accordance with the law of his nature. Every baby is a new being with a nature of his own, and what was good for his brother may not be good for him. The training that will give one child self-confidence will make a little tyrant of another; what would render one merely amenable to control might make a coward of another. So you see, my dear, that a mother needs to have great knowledge of the laws of mind and great insight in the applying of those laws to the particular cases she has in hand."

"It really seems, mamma, as if girls ought to study all those things before they marry."

"Indeed they ought, but I fear they never will until they come to have a clearer idea of the value and importance of the mother's work. When they realize that the great and lasting work of the world  is done in the homes, by the mothers, with their little children, then we shall have men demanding that girls shall be prepared for that important work by previous education.

"There is another way, too, in which women are given great power over the destiny of the world, and that is through heredity."

"What does that word mean, mother? I have heard it very often, but people speak as if it were something undesirable."

"Heredity means the passing on of traits or talents from parents to children. Now, your eyes are like papa's. They are a part of your heredity from him. You have other features like him, and you have many of his traits. It has been easy to teach you to be orderly because you have inherited his love of order. Then, too, you have many of my characteristics. My hair, my love of music, my quick temper."

Helen looked at her mother somewhat in surprise.

"Do you mean, mamma, that I have a quick temper because you had one?"

"I certainly do; and if I had known, when I was of your age, what I know now, I might have given you a different disposition."

"Will my children have a temper because I have one?"

"There will be a greater probability of their having quick tempers because you have one."

"How can I help it, if I got my temper from  you and just passed it on to them? Certainly I am not to blame."

"Many people excuse themselves for their faults in just that way; but that is to give evil greater power than good, and we don't believe in that, you know. Each one has the power to make himself over, and in the process he may change the direction of the inheritance of his children."

"You mean that if I overcome my temper, my children will not be so likely to have tempers?"

"Yes, by controlling yourself you will have given them greater power of self-control; that is worth working for, isn't it? If, when I was of your age, I had begun to govern my temper, I should have been helping you. So it is in every field of effort. If you are a good student and cultivate your mental powers to the best of your ability, you will make it easier for your children to be good students. Now, in your young girlhood, you are working to help future generations."

"But maybe I'll never have any children, mamma; what then?"

"None of us can see our future, but if we are wise we will prepare for the probabilities. At your age I could not be sure that I would ever be a mother, and now I have several children to call forth every power that I possess through inheritance or by education. You are not sorry that in many ways I was wise enough so to cultivate myself that you have inherited desirable qualities; and you have cause to regret that I did not know  now to do better for you. You can learn through my failures, and be kinder to your children than I have been to you. I can assure you of one thing,—even if you never have children, you will never regret having cultivated yourself in every talent and virtue, but you may have great cause for sorrow if you fail to develop the best in yourself. There is no grief in the world like that caused by wilful or wicked sons and daughters. Their waywardness brings not only sorrow but self-condemnation on the parents who must feel that in some way they have been to blame, either in the inheritance they passed on or the training they gave. And there is no happiness equal to the just pride felt in honorable children. As Solomon says: 'Children's children are the crown of old men, and the glory of children are their fathers.'"

Helen was silent a moment and then asked, "Don't you think the law of heredity a very cruel law? It doesn't seem fair that children should be punished for the sins of their parents."

"God's laws are never cruel, dear. They are always made for our good, and they will be for our good, if we use them rightly. Harry Severn fell yesterday from a scaffold and broke his leg because of the law of gravitation. You might say that was a cruel law, and that God was unkind to make such a law whereby we can be so seriously injured. But think for one moment what that law means in the universe. If it were not for this  mysterious force which we call gravitation, the whole creation would be in chaos. Nothing would stay in place, buildings could not be made, people would fly off the earth and go, no one knows whither. Why, all the suns, moons, and stars of the universe are held in place by gravitation. If we are ever hurt through the action of that law it is because we were not happily related to it, that is all. The law is good, and what we have to do is to learn to work with it.

"It is just so with this law of heredity. It is the law of transmission. It works right along and transmits good or evil. It is our part to relate ourselves to it so that it will transmit mostly good. When we come to think of it, we see that that is what it principally does. Health, and honesty, and virtue, all good traits, are so constantly transmitted that we do not think of their coming through heredity, just as we do not think of all order and stability coming through gravity; but when undesirable traits are inherited we complain of the law, just as we complain when we are hurt through the law of gravitation. But do you not see that it is the very fact that the law is sure, that it invariably transmits evil, is one guarantee of its surety in transmitting good? Indeed, the Bible tells us that good is transmitted in greater degree than evil. The third commandment gives us the law of heredity: 'For I, the Lord thy God, am a jealous God, visiting the iniquities of the fathers upon the children to the third and fourth  generation of them that hate me and showing mercy unto thousands of them that love me and keep my commandments.' That does not mean thousands of individuals, but, as the revised version gives it, 'thousands of generations.' So you see what encouragement this law gives us. The evil in us is to be transient, the good everlasting. Instead of being weighed down by our undesirable inheritances, we should be encouraged to overcome them and to cultivate our good ones."

"Mamma, don't you think the fathers have something to do as well as the mothers, in trying to give a better inheritance to the children?"

"I surely do, and that is where I think a girl needs to be especially wise in the choice of a husband. If a man has traits or habits that she would not want her children to have, she should remember that, through the law of heredity, that trait is one they will be very likely to inherit.

"Girls quite often think it does not matter if a young man smokes, or even if he drinks a little, but when we study heredity we see what a threat such habits are to the health and welfare of his children. I remember when John Orland was a handsome young man, he drank, sometimes to excess. Kittie Claiborne knew this, and her friends opposed her marrying him, but she thought she could reform him, and you know the result. Her husband is a confirmed drunkard, as is her youngest son. The oldest drinks, too, though not to such excess, and you know that Kitty Orland, such a beautiful girl, has more than once been found under the influence of liquor. The second girl died of consumption, and the second son is weak-minded."

"But, mamma, do you mean that this is all because Mr. Orland drinks?"

"The observation of scientific men as to the effects of alcohol through inheritance would lead us to think so. I find this little item in the paper. You may read it."

Helen read—

"European scientists have recently given much attention to the physical degradation among children which they believe to be the result of intemperance on the part of the parents. A startling example was recently published in the London Daily News:

"Some months ago a workman and his wife, accompanied by a small boy of four, waited on Doctor Garnier, the physician who presides over the insanity ward at the Paris Depot, or Central Police Station. The parents were in great distress, and the story they had to tell was that on two occasions the lad, their son, who was with them, had attempted to murder his baby brother. On the last occasion the mother had just arrived in time to prevent him from cutting the baby's throat with a pair of scissors.

"Examined by Doctor Garnier, the child declared it was quite true that he wished to murder his brother, and that it was his firm intention to accomplish his purpose, sooner or later.

"Taking the parents into an adjoining room, Doctor Garnier said to the father, 'Are you a drinker?'

"The man protested indignantly. He had never been drunk in his life. His wife backed up his assertion. Her husband, she said, was the most sober of men.

"'Hold out your hand at arm's length,' said the doctor.

"The man obeyed. After a few seconds the hand began that devil's dance to which alcohol fiddles the tune.

"'As I thought,' said the doctor. 'My poor fellow, you are an alcoholique.'

"He questioned the man, who, with tears in his eyes, related that, being a brewer's drayman, it was his duty to deliver casks of beer to his master's customers, carrying the casks up to various stages. A glass of wine was occasionally offered him as a pouboire. The total quantity so absorbed by him amounted to a liter, or a liter and a half per day. This had been going on steadily for several years.

"'With the result,' said the doctor, 'that you, who have never been drunk, have become so completely alcoholized that you have transmitted to that unfortunate baby in the next room a form of epilepsy which has developed into homicidal mania.'"

"Isn't it awful, mamma? I should not want to marry a man who drinks."

"I sincerely hope you never will. But there are other habits that are evil in their effects. Smoking, for example."

"O, mamma, smoking isn't inherited, is it?"

"Well, I don't know but we might say that it is. I knew a woman who was an inveterate smoker. When her baby was born, it cried night and day until one day the mother, nearly distracted, took the pipe from her mouth and put it between the baby's lips and it stopped crying at once, and after that she took that method to still its cries. You see, it had been under the influence of tobacco all the time before it was born, and when it no longer felt that influence it was uncomfortable until it had the tobacco again. You know how hard it is for a man to give up smoking. All poisons by long use make such an impression on the body that it suffers when the poisons are taken away.

"Tobacco paralyzes the nerves of sensation, so that feeling is lessened. That is why men like to use it. They think they feel better, when in reality they feel less, or not at all; and to have no feeling or power to feel is a dangerous condition. Pain, or sensation, is our great protection, and to remove sensation by paralysis is to render ourselves open to danger. This paralytic condition may become an inheritance. Many children have  infantile paralysis because their fathers are users of tobacco.”

“I am glad my father doesn’t use it,” exclaimed Helen with emphasis.

“Indeed, you may well be glad, and you can see to it that your children have the same cause for rejoicing. The girls of to-day have a wonderful influence on all time, the present and the future. I wish they knew how to use it wisely.”

“But girls think it is manly to smoke. I’ve heard lots of them say so. Stella Wilson says she wouldn’t marry a man that didn’t smoke; and Kate Barrows said the other day that she thought girls had no right to interfere with the enjoyment of men by asking them to give up smoking. She said she knew how nice it was, for she had tried it; and she said the most fashionable women smoke, and she means to smoke when she has a home of her own.”

“All of which only proves that she is a poor, ignorant girl who does not know her own value to herself, or to the world. She may yet have cause to weep over children made weak and nervous, or who have died because of her ignorance.”

“Isn’t it sad that ignorance does not save us from punishment?”

“Yes, but it does not. If you can’t swim, you may drown, even while trying to save another. God’s laws cannot vary to save us from the penalty of ignorance.

“I wonder now, dear, if you are not beginning to see the greatness of woman’s work. In her own vigor she creates health for the future of the nation. So you see whether you wear your overshoes or not, may be a question of importance to the race. By her virtue, courage, patience, purity, she is storing up those qualities for the men and women of the future. By her demanding of her future husband that he shall be without fear and without reproach, as clean in life and thought as herself, she is building up protections around the children of generations to come. Even the young girls of to-day are creating national conditions for the future, are deciding the destiny of the nation,—yes, of the race. The great structures that men build will in time perish, but character is eternal. Is it not even a greater thing to be a woman than to be a man?”

“I begin to think so, and I think after this I’ll try to feel that even I am of importance to the world, instead of regretting that I am not a man.”